PUN DIRECTION

STEWART FRANCIS

OVER **500** OF HIS GREATEST GAGS ...AND FOUR CRAP ONES!

headline

First published in 2013 by
HEADLINE PUBLISHING GROUP

1

Cataloguing in Publication Data
is available from the British Library

Hardback ISBN 978 0 7553 6578 4

Typeset in Serifa and Oklahoma

Printed and bound in Great Britain by
Clays Ltd, St Ives plc

Headline's policy is to use papers that are natural,
renewable and recyclable products and made from wood
grown in sustainable forests. The logging and manufacturing
processes are expected to conform to the environmental
regulations of the country of origin.

HEADLINE PUBLISHING GROUP
An Hachette UK Company
338 Euston Road
London NW1 3BH

www.headline.co.uk
www.hachette.co.uk

This book is deducted to
all my spelling teachers

• • • • • • • • • • • •

'Keep your face to the sunshine and you cannot see a shadow'
Helen Keller

• • • • • • • • • • • •

• • • • • • • • • • • •

'Dial Before You Dig'
National Grid

• • • • • • • • • • • •

CHAPTER ONE

ALL OF LENNY HENRY'S BEST JOKES

CHAPTER TWO

ALL OF MY BEST JOKES

．．．．．．．．．．．．．．

I'm the youngest of three,
my parents are both older.

I have mixed race parents,
my father prefers the 100 metres.

I farted in a full lift today,
which was wrong on so
many levels.

It's thought that most men's sexual fantasy is to be involved in a threesome and I thought it was mine until recently when I WAS involved in a threesome. I'll be honest with you, I didn't like it. Halfway through I stopped and said 'Listen Rick, Jim...'

I couldn't be gay...
         I just don't have it in me.

The best fancy dress prize was down to me, dressed like the *Titanic*, and another person.
I was a nervous wreck.

I think the guy who designed the thong is a bit up his own arse.

I'm not a very competitive person and I'm always the first to say it.

I'm not very good
at hide-and-seek,
I think you'll find.

Never play hide-and-seek
with a Peking duck.
    Cheating bastards.

Unfortunately for agoraphobics,
a cure is just around the corner.

. . . .

I'm not a driven man,
    which is why I'm usually late.

I was once late because of
    high-fiving a centipede.

A badly timed high-five is
    a real slap in the face.

. . . . PD . . . . . .

I've been called too vague by
you-know-who.

I'm a paranoid schizophrenic but
you know what they say.
           What are they saying?!

I hate indecisive people.
      Well, hate is a strong word,
      it's more that I don't like
      indecisive people.
           Actually, it's not that
           I don't like them...

• • • • • • • • • • • • • • • • •

I've been called a hypochondriac,
which really hurts.

A lot of people call me old-fashioned
...poppycock.

I've been called irritating
not once, not twice, not
three times, not four times,
not five times, not six times,
not seven times, not eight
times, not even nine times,
not ten times, not eleven
times, not twelve times, not
thirteen times, not fourteen
times, not fifteen times...

• • • • • • • • 🅿🅳 • • • • • •

AFTER 21 YEARS IN BUSINESS TOGETHER,
ANDY AND BILL DECIDE TO CUT TIES

There was a documentary about kids with weird names that I watched with keen interest. And Keen Interest said to me, 'Daddy, where's Venezuela?' I said, 'she should be home right after lacrosse practice', and just then, who walks in? And behind Who...

Lacrosse Practice.

You should always know
your facts. That's what the
late Dolly Parton used to
always say, before she
was killed in Vietnam...
damn you O.J. Simpson.

Oh, what a tangled web
we weave, when first we
practice to deceive...
I wrote that.

With so much nudity on T.V.
I just sit there, shaking my fist.
            Last night I was furious.

I'm not an expert on
masturbation,
            but I hold my own.

            There's nothing weird about
masturbation, it's perfectly natural.
            I remember the first time my
parents found me masturbating.
            I wasn't ashamed, I was more
startled. I almost dropped their
            wedding picture.

• • • • • • • • • • • • • • • •

Do I sometimes get my
sayings mixed up?
　　　　　Does the Pope shit
　　　　　　in the woods?

I perform self-deprecating comedy.
　　Although, I'm not very good at it.

Have you ever noticed
how popular observational
comedy is?

　　　I think bad spellers
　　should form an onion.

• • • • • • • ✎ • • • • • • •

When I was a kid my parents told me that they were too poor to buy me a skateboard. So one night, I tippy-toed out of my bedroom, got a piece of wood and a hammer and I beat them to death.

My nervous foster parents bought me five skateboards.

Q & ~~A~~ Eh?

If you could have dinner with anyone dead or alive, who would it be?
   Someone alive.

Which stop should I get off at for the Bentall Shopping Centre?
   Cromwell Road.

What did you say to the Olympic fencer who stole your wife?
   Touché.

You've been described as having a limited attention span whereby you'll often leave someone mid-conversation. Is that true?

Your father was a plumber and your mother was a choreographer. What did they want you to be?
   A tap dancer.

When did you first realise that you were a hypochondriac?
   Shortly after my first period.

18

• • • • • • • • • • • • • • • • • •

Your wife is expecting to give birth to twins imminently.
Where will you be on that special day?
  Thailand.

When did you know that you would never do a pun
about dentists?
  2:30.

Boxers or briefs?
  A true gentleman would never reveal such
  information. I was taught that by my mother
  (36-28-34).

Who is your favourite singer?
  Peter Andre.

Do you have any physical impairments?
  I have tinnitus.

Where did your parents tell you that you were adopted? ✓
  In our igloo.

Studies suggest that women are sexually aroused by men
with foreign accents. Do you agree?
  Absolutamente.

• • • • • • • • • • • • • • • •

I'd like to dedicate this book to
my father, who was a roofer.
　　　So dad, if you're up there…

I was raised by my father,
　　　my mother left before
　　　　　　　I was born.

I liked being raised by my
father, he's schizophrenic, but
he's good people.
　　　I remember one summer
　　　when I was five
　　　　　and he was Mussolini.

• • • • • • • • PD • • • • • • • •

Growing up, I was always under the impression that my father didn't like me very much because we hardly ever did anything together. We only went fishing once, and I remember swimming back to shore thinking...

We only went golfing once, and I remember swimming back to shore thinking, 'Golf's a lot like fishing, and, my father doesn't like me very much'.

My dad took off when I was about ten years old and it turns out he's a trucking Mormon.
No, he's a fucking moron.

Over the years, so many people
have jumped on the Barack
Obama bandwagon, which, as an
African American, offends me.

They say if you're nervous
that you should picture the
audience naked...
            unless you're doing
            a kids' show.

My impression of an
after-dinner speaker at
a bulimia convention:
'Hey, where's everyone going?'

They say you shouldn't
make fun of the blind...
                    watch me.

I remember the first time my
father took me trick-or-treating.
I remember swimming back to
shore thinking, 'Snoopy costumes
are heavy when they're wet'.

Because of ridiculous
stereotypes, people can
be so ignorant towards
other nationalities.
I'm thin, I don't play the
banjo and I don't fuck my
cousin, yet still, people
assume that I'm American.
What's that all aboot?

I'm a very proud Canadian
who's very proud of the
education system in Canadia.
I think it's the goodest
of all seventeen countries.

ED MEETS WITH HIS SILENT PARTNERS

I was terrible at school. I failed maths so many times, I can't even count.

I was good at history.
  Wait a minute, no, no I wasn't.

In school, the other kids used to push me and call me lazy...
        I loved that wheelchair.

  I preferred French over chemistry because the chemistry teacher and I just didn't have any... rapport.

One teacher said that I would be
a better student if I spent less time
flirting. I immediately jumped off
his lap and ran as fast as I could,
which isn't easy in stilettos.

In high school I was voted most likely
to reminisce. Ahhhhhh, good times.

In school, one teacher used to
always say that I wasn't very
observant, but you know what,
that was only his or her opinion.

Another teacher said that I was
incapable of retaining information.
Me, Stewart Fletcher.

I pride myself on doing a great job
as I'm a real prefectionist.

√ Sadly, I don't speak French…
                    such is life.

I went to a French restaurant
where I was served by a very
ugly waitress.
          She gave me the crêpes.

NOT MUCH WAS WRITTEN ABOUT
PAVLOV'S EVIL TWIN BROTHER STAN

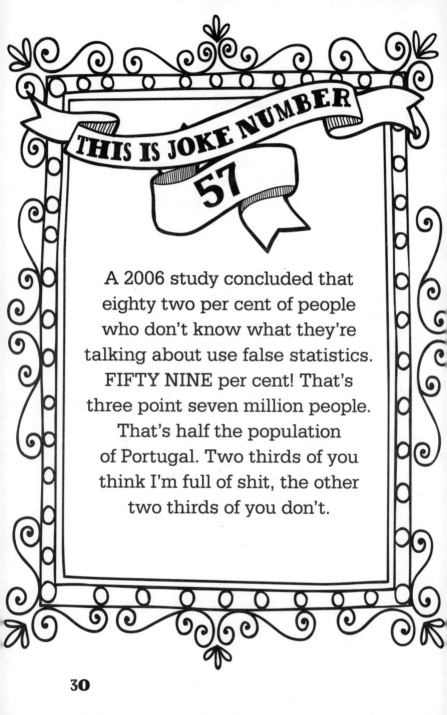

A 2006 study concluded that
eighty two per cent of people
who don't know what they're
talking about use false statistics.
FIFTY NINE per cent! That's
three point seven million people.
That's half the population
of Portugal. Two thirds of you
think I'm full of shit, the other
two thirds of you don't.

The Chuckle Brothers might
be funny to you, to me...

Correct me if I'm wrong, but
people who say, 'Correct me
if I'm wrong' seldom are.
That's why they say it –
they know they're right.
You never hear someone
saying, 'Correct me if
I'm wrong, but, a kitten
invented the steam engine.'

. . . .

I like my women the way
I like my coffee.
    Picked by migrant workers.

Women are attracted to bad boys.
        I read that in prison.
            In a magazine I stole...
                from the warden.

A beautiful woman could
move a mountain.
        Actually, she'd get a man
        to move the mountain
        and then she'd bitch
        about where he put it.

. . . . PD . . . .

My girlfriend thinks that
I'm afraid of commitment.
      Well, she's not really
      my girlfriend.

My girlfriend thinks that I'm
incapable of being faithful.
   My wife on the other hand...
   has a sister I wouldn't mind...
      if you know what I mean.

A friend of mine doesn't know how to do the 'if you know what I mean' thing. He'll say to me, 'I'm going to go home and slide my penis into my wife's vagina… if you know what I mean'.

A good time to wink is after you say something cheeky.
A bad time to wink is after you say 'I'm not a racist, but…'

A BRUNCH WITH DEATH

My father was a man of few words.
I remember he used to say to me,
'Son . . . . get your trunks,
we're going to the library.'

Like most deaf people,
my father went to the
school of hard knocks.

The best advice I ever
received from my father was
that you can never run away
from your problems. And to this
day, I still have that postcard.
New Zealand sure looks lovely.

My dad used to say 'A man
should never be ashamed of
what he does for a living.'
He would then put on a clown
costume and go to work.
Arguably, the worst
lawyer ever.

I don't think I got the job
at Microsoft.
They haven't responded
to my telegram.

I was a mime.
        It's only now that
        I can talk about it.

I was a trapeze artist
            but I was let go.

I was a trampoline salesman,
                off and on.

            I was a glass blower
            but then Mr. Glass
            was transferred.

I was fired as a taxidermist
for doing a half-assed job.

I used to install mirrors,
which was something I could
always see myself doing.

I quit my job as a psychic.
I just couldn't see a future in it.

My wife is an unemployed
stool sample technician.
She's between jobbies.

SHOULD HE EVER NEED ANYTHING,
THE ANDERSONS LET THEIR NEW
NEIGHBOUR MERV KNOW THAT THEY'RE
JUST A STONE'S THROW AWAY

That's the thing my friends,
I'm a one-liner comedian.
I'm NOT a story teller
and it's funny how that all started...

I tried phone sex recently and got
my phone bill just the other day.
EIGHT HUNDRED AND FIFTY
THREE POUNDS.
Man, don't call 'Stuttering Sluts'.

They now have a website for
stutterers, it's wwwdotwww
dotwwwdotwwwdotdotdot.

Do homeless people really get knock-knock jokes?

I went to university on a . . . . . . swimming scholarship.

At university I was going to join the debating team, but someone talked me out of it.

I don't know how to say this so
I'm going to say something else.

There's a fine line between
hyphenated words.

I give evolution two thumbs up.

A teacher, who was convinced that
I didn't know what a simile was,
had a face like the back of a boat.
                        And she was stern.

I read that ten out of two people are dyslexic.

I hope that dyslexics are accepted here in the KU.

A friend of mine is a dyslexic chef.
Don't order the carp,
it tastes like shit.

I don't do puns about firing squads.

Shoot me.

I like to go to bookstores and say to the clerk, 'I'm looking for a book titled "How to Deal with Rejection Without Killing", do you have it?'

When I was a kid, my dad used to always hit me with a camera. I still have flashbacks.

When I was a kid, my fairy godmother asked me if I wanted a long penis or a long memory. I forget my response.

I think women who think size doesn't matter are shallow.

I wasn't circumcised,
   I was circumnavigated.

The more someone boasts about
something, the less likely it's true.
      I'll never forget the day
      my huge cock told me that.

My sexual fantasy is to make love
      to Sigmund Freud's father...
                  MOTHER.

BUOYS WILL BE BUOYS

• • • • • • • • • • • • • • • •

I used to drive a Ford Focus
but, er, ah, um… sorry.

I now drive an Echo.
You heard me, I said Echo.

You know you're driving a piece
of shit when a hitchhiker says to
you, 'Ah, actually, no thanks.'

• • • • • • • • PD • • • • • • •

There's not enough respect
in this world as I'm sure
you idiots would agree.

Imagine discriminating against
someone simply because of the
colour of their skin. Try putting
yourself in their shoes, or whatever
the hell it is that they wear on their
feet. What's up with that anyway?
LET'S GET THEM.

You know what, I don't care if
you're white, I don't care if you're
black, I don't care if you're Asian,
I DON'T CARE ABOUT YOU.

You should never book a
holiday when you're hungry.
That's not to say that I didn't
enjoy Turkey and Brussels. *spout*

I recently went to Sweden.
I've always wanted to
go to Sweden, ever since
I was a little girl.*

I recently went to Bangkok
where men are men...
                and so are women.

*At the time this joke was written Sweden was known
 as the sex-change capital of the world.

I went to Birmingham
with low expectations
and left disappointed.

A lot of people prefer
Birmingham in the summer.
        I prefer it in the rear
        view mirror.

Even though I'm proud of my father
for inventing the rear view mirror,
we're not as close as we appear.

They say opposites attract,
but try explaining that
to my short, ugly wife.

I did a show for a group of
backpackers.
They were sitting on
the edge of their seats.

And if you don't like a backpacking
joke, put it behind you...
take a hike.

AT HOME WITH HANDSOME ACTOR SAM,
WHO HAS ALWAYS BEEN A SCENE STEALER

I recently auditioned for
the part of Jesus Christ...
nailed it.

Is religion about making money?
I don't know, ask a prophet.

My uncle is easily the most
devout Catholic I have ever
~~been touched by~~ met.

My uncle was crushed by a piano.
His funeral was very low key.
B flat.

I was at a book signing today.
I'll tell you, librarians have no
sense of humour.

A part of me feels I
can be too candid.
Another part of me
is my bum hole.

CULTURE VULTURES

I read that a hunter in America
shot and killed a man that he
mistook to be an elk. He had
a difficult time explaining to
the police what he thought an
elk was doing in a motel room,
fucking his wife.

Also in the States,
a man robbed an art class.
Police now have 22
sketches of the robber.
　　　　Fortunately for the robber
　　　　it was a surrealist art class.
　　　　　　Police are looking for a
　　　　　　3-legged coffee table.

Irony:
I once slapped a homeless
person so hard, my charm
bracelet fell off.

Irony:
Sharon Osborne
judges talent.

Irony:
There's a paper in Britain
called *The Sun*.

A recently divorced friend
of mine is hopeful of once
again finding romance.
Beer-bellied, completely bald,
I don't like her chances.
And the lazy eye doesn't help.

I was involved in a one-night
stand that went horribly wrong.
        We've been married
        three years now.

My wife and I are at the stage
in our marriage where we're
starting to finish each other's
… drinks.

We're always arguing over the
little things, which she'd prefer I
didn't call our midget neighbours.

My wife is beautiful.
My wife has an ass like J-Lo…
no, jello.

My wife is from Scotland.
We've been married for three
years and I have not understood
a single word she has said.

I'm not ashamed of my wife.
If you don't believe me, go out
to the car and ask her.

Ask her loud,
she's in the boot.

A lot of churches won't let
you throw confetti, which
put a real damper on my...
mom's funeral.

My wife and I have decided
that we don't want children.
If anyone does, we can drop
them off tomorrow.

Actually, we have a beautiful
little girl who we named after
my mother. In fact Passive
Aggressive Psycho turns five
tomorrow.

I just hope my kids don't become
cynical like their father,
whoever he is.

Is my wife dissatisfied
with my body?
A tiny part of me says yes.

Every joke has a victim, it depends
on your perspective as to who that
victim is. I once did a joke about
Christopher Reeve, unaware of the
fact that in the audience was a man
in a wheelchair who clearly did not
find the joke funny. Behind him was
a table of horses that thought it was
fucking hilarious.

My wife and I met at a castanet
class, where we just clicked.

No, we're both tightrope walkers,
                    we met online.

No, we actually met in a museum,
                    and the rest is history.

No, we actually met
at a driving range,
where we hit it off.

Truthfully, we met at a chess match,
        where she made the first move.

No, we actually met in a library,
that's novel.

No, we really met at the
Wright Brothers Museum.
It was love at first flight.

No, we met at high school.
She was fifteen and I was...
dropping off my grandson.

No, we met at a mystery
novel convention.
Or did we?

• • • • • • • • • • • • • • • •

No, first we met at a wicker store.
We were basket cases.

No, we met at a fertility clinic.
I just loved her spunk.

No, we met at a retro club
and we haven't looked back.

No, no, no, truth be told,
we met at the Special Olympics,
it was a no-brainer.

I'm only kidding, I'm only kidding…
I'm not married.

• • • • • • • 𝓟𝓓 • • • • • • • •

I was previously married.
I married way too young.
A Chinese girl, that's her name.

Way too young was so
beautiful. Fab cook too,
that was her cousin.

It was a good-looking family.
So so hot, she was the ugly one.
I could never figure that one out.

Way too young ended
up marrying a Chinese
billionaire... ka ching.

THE
Agony
Uncle
With Uncle Stewie

Dear Stewie

I had a drunken snog with a friend's husband
and now I feel guilty whenever I see them.
I'm mortified that I've ruined a great
friendship with a stupid, drunken kiss.

Stewie Says: You think that's bad,
my sciatica is so painful in my left calf that
whenever I stand up it feels like a lightning
bolt shooting down my leg. I can only pee
whilst sitting down. Hope that helps you.

Dear Stewie

I'm a man of 32 and I'm in love with a 17-year-
old girl, is there something the matter with me?

Stewie Says: Funny you should mention.

I've got irritable bowel syndrome which sometimes gets so bad that I double over in pain and weep like a baby person. Let me know how it turns out.

Dear Stewie

Since the birth of my second child I haven't been able to lose any of the weight that I gained during my pregnancy. I'm okay with my body but my husband constantly makes fun of it, especially in social situations. How can I get him to stop?

Stewie Says: I'm sorry to hear that. I've developed arthritis in both hands which is so bad at times that it prohibits me from participating in my favourite hobby, pot holing. Keep me posted.

This has been the Agony Uncle *with Uncle Stewie*

I don't know where it all went
wrong with me and my last
girlfriend, or tubby, as I called her.

For some reason, she had
really low self-esteem.
And saggy tits…
        as I called her.

She wasn't very attractive,
but like my grandma used to
always say, 'You don't fuck the face.'
        No wait, she'd say, 'Fancy
        another biscuit?'
                I don't know why I
                always got those two
                sayings mixed up.

IT'S ALL KICKED OFF IN THE MIDDLE EAST AGAIN

THE POUND SHOT UP TODAY

TOPICAL FISH

I guess what I'm trying to
say is that I'm a romantic.
I'm such a romantic, I
remember my very first date.
  My father came along and
  acted as a chaperone, which
  was awkward, because my
  date couldn't swim.

You can tell the quality of a person
  by what that person does in their
  spare time. Once a week, I like to
go over to the local orphanage and
  yell 'Who's your daddy?'... 'Mom's
    the word'... 'Bob's your uncle'.
        Yep, you do what you can.

Once a week, I like to take
a whistle to train stations...
old people run funny.

Prior to moving to the UK I lived
in Spain. I lived in a traditional
village that still has cock fights...
which explains my limp.

Two types of people I hate
are racists... and Norwegians.
Especially the black ones.

. . . .

My wife said to me, 'You're
not very compassionate about
the fact that I'm diabetic.'
        I said, 'Sugar... honey...
        sweetie... insulin'.

        I love being in a committed
                marriage so much that I'll
                        probably do it again.

I am faithfully married, that's why
I'm wearing this wedding ring.
        OOPS, um, it must have fallen
        off in that hooker's ass...
        what am I like?

. . . . PD . . . .

You really find out about someone AFTER you marry them.

For example, my wife doesn't have a 'PEANUT' allergy, no, no it turns out she has a 'PENIS'...

that's it, she has a penis.

I tried that psychological test on my wife. I said, 'Honey, is a glass half full or half empty?' She said, 'I don't give a fuck, but if it's on the coffee table, there better be a fucking coaster under it.'

My wife says I do too many stereotypical jokes…

huh… women.

As the saying goes:
'Women – can't live with them…'
That's it, you can't live with them.

As a Canadian, I like to go clubbing.
But if there are no seals around…
I like to go dancing.

Money-wise, I'm set for life.
Provided I die next Tuesday.

To me, gambling is like
a midget at a barbeque.
Oftentimes, the steaks
are too high.

There's a guy in my neighbourhood
who's in the *Guinness Book of Records*
for having forty-three concussions.
He lives very close, in fact,
just a stone's throw away.

I've been a little depressed of late.
Just last week I noticed that I
have a grey pubic hair. But I was
okay with it, I didn't freak out…
          unlike the others in the lift.

        I saw a chiropodist today.
        Either I have ugly feet or
he has Tourette's Syndrome.

I was addicted to rolling
around in pig shit.
I've been clean for two years now.

My doctor thinks that I'm
taking hallucinogenic drugs.
How do I know?
Let's just say a little
bird told me.

They're building an IKEA in my
neighbourhood. Every time I go
by I feel sorry for the builders.
They're like, 'Where the hell
does this piece go?'

IKEA is a Swedish
word for 'FUCK!'

My therapist says that I have a
preoccupation with vengeance...
we'll see about that.

He also says that I have
an overactive imagination,
or, something to that effect.
I was distracted by the
tap-dancing chipmunks
on his water cooler.

I was called immature today
by my smelly wife...
so I spat on her.

Receiving oral sex from an ugly
person is like rock climbing...
    you should never look down.

Success really does change people.
I used to be a very self-conscious
                waitress from Swindon,
                    now look at me...
                    don't look at me.

I'm going to level with you.
I'm not a certified bricklayer.

Having this book published
makes me wish that both my
parents were still...
                    interested in my career.

                    People say I have the legs of a
                    dancer. But, until they find the
                    rest of the body, the cops got
                                nothin' on me, man.

When women see me naked,
they often say that I look like
a Greek god. I think his name
is Hermaphrodite.

Someone recently called me
a shameless self-promoter. **ME**...
Stewart Francis... **dot com**!

I've been described as being
dismissive and having a limited
vocabulary... huh... sheesh...
phfft... women.

People say that I'm a plagiarist...
their word, not mine.

I've been called a terrible
name-dropper by my
best friend, **KEVIN LOGIE**.

I haven't said a silly word in
...yonks.

I have never asked a rhetorical
question. How cool is that?

Today, I squatted down,
put my head between my
legs and fell forward.
That's how I roll.

My ex-girlfriend said we can work
on my bladder problem together.
I said, 'There is no wee.'

My uncle just set a new world
record by getting twenty-seven
pigeons to land on him.
What a ledge.
They should make a
statue of that man.

Does my wife think
I'm a control freak?
I haven't decided yet.

She used to hate that joke...
and now she loves it.
I just had to stare
at her long enough.

The other night at a party,
my wife got drunk and told
everyone that she invented
the echo.
 I said, 'Listen to yourself.'

 Unfortunately, the blueprint to
 my honey farm was destroyed.
 I have no plan B.

I'm considered to be the
inventor of the hula-hoop
in some circles.

There's a guy on Facebook
that keeps saying all my
plates are chipped.
There's a woman on Bebo
that keeps saying all my
cutlery is tarnished.
There's a guy on Twitter
that keeps saying my
gravy boat is tacky.
Has anyone else been the
victim of a sideboard bully?

To me, Ed Miliband doesn't look
like a leader. To me, Ed Miliband
looks like a security guard who just
heard a noise in the warehouse.

My mother's my best friend,
which some people think is weird.
'Creepy' is the term one motel
manager used.

Fat people block the pavement.
There's no getting around it.

My next-door neighbour
is a deaf soul singer....
SAY WHAT?

THEIR INITIAL MEETING

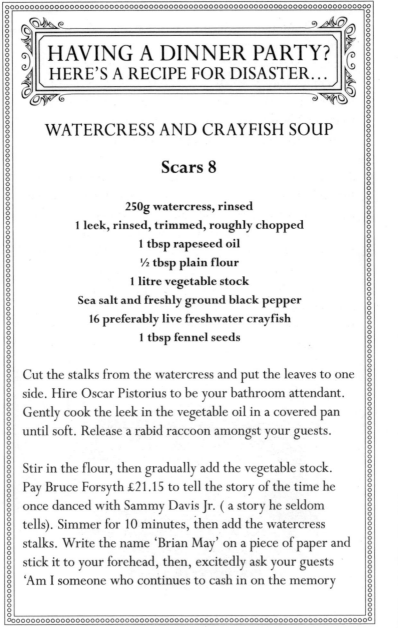

HAVING A DINNER PARTY?
HERE'S A RECIPE FOR DISASTER…

WATERCRESS AND CRAYFISH SOUP

Scars 8

250g watercress, rinsed
1 leek, rinsed, trimmed, roughly chopped
1 tbsp rapeseed oil
½ tbsp plain flour
1 litre vegetable stock
Sea salt and freshly ground black pepper
16 preferably live freshwater crayfish
1 tbsp fennel seeds

Cut the stalks from the watercress and put the leaves to one side. Hire Oscar Pistorius to be your bathroom attendant. Gently cook the leek in the vegetable oil in a covered pan until soft. Release a rabid raccoon amongst your guests.

Stir in the flour, then gradually add the vegetable stock. Pay Bruce Forsyth £21.15 to tell the story of the time he once danced with Sammy Davis Jr. (a story he seldom tells). Simmer for 10 minutes, then add the watercress stalks. Write the name 'Brian May' on a piece of paper and stick it to your forehead, then, excitedly ask your guests 'Am I someone who continues to cash in on the memory of Freddie Mercury?' Remove from the heat, add two-thirds of the watercress leaves. Activate your Strongbow fountain. Strain through a fine-meshed sieve, not too fine as it becomes watery. Pay Bruce Forsyth £16.28 to repeat his hilarious catchphrase (which he seldom does). Bring back to the boil briefly and season again with salt and pepper. Release Charles Saatchi amongst your guests.

To cook the crayfish, bring a pan of heavily salted water to the boil and simmer for 5 minutes. Turn up the thermostat, and invite Brian Blessed and Eamonn Holmes over to play Twister. Drop in the crayfish, simmer for 3-4 minutes. Play the DVD *The Human Centipede*. Remove the tail meat by pulling away the heads and squeezing the shells until they crack. Read an entire chapter from Katie Price's 39th, and arguably worst, book. Next, add the crayfish meat to the soup and serve. After dinner, get George Michael to drive your guests home.

BON APPETIT

● ● ● ● ● ● ● ● ● ● ● ● ● ● ● ● ●

People who reinforce
negative stereotypes…
what's that all aboot?

Negative stereotypes get me so
angry that I just want to throw
down my jar of maple syrup, crawl
out of my igloo, pick up an ice
hockey stick and club a seal…
or a moose… or Justin Bieber.
You're welcome.

I'm Canadian, but I'm sure
that most of you have already
figured that oot.

● ● ● ● ● ● ● PD ● ● ● ● ● ●

I'm a member of an
organization called H.B.R,
Canadians Against Dyslexia.

This year, we had
our conference in Mali,
although most of us
went to Lima.

One idiot went to Albuquerque.
            Which, I really enjoyed.

Canada has the fewest number of pretentious people to speak Latin than anywhere else in the world... per capita.

I come from a small town in Canada. The town is so small I'm the barbershop quartet.

My uncle once ejaculated on me. I'm glad I got that off my chest.

THE BEAR OF BAD NEWS

I've been accused of doing nothing but sitting around all day watching hip hop videos by my... bitch.

Shorty's all up in my grill.
My boo's just trippin',
she knows my flava's hot.
I have no idea what I just said.
           And that's fo' shizzle.

I do watch a lot of television.
    The entire screen for that matter.

I watched a documentary on
how ships are held together...
riveting.

I watched a show called *Last of the
Summer Wine*. If you haven't seen
it, it's about three creepy old guys
who roam the countryside, trying
to be funny and failing miserably.
Wait, I meant *Top Gear*.

I've got a joke about Moses
that will divide the room.

 I've got a joke about cannibalism
which, ironically, is in good taste.

One thing that I won't joke
about is illiteracy. Because
'r' there's nothing funny about
illiteracy, 'h' it's rude...

Puns about air conditioners?
Not a fan.

I have never and will never
do a pun about erections.
Touch wood.

Am I cynical about religion?
Is the Pope…
        protecting paedophiles?

I don't think my wife being very
religious will have an impact on our
two daughters, Samantha and…
                John the Baptist.

I met my wife in Bangkok.
And no, she's not a lady-boy.
Although my razor blade is
always dull. And she'll only do anal.
Which always hurts my bum.

Anal sex, or as my uncle
calls it… 'shhhhhhhhh'.

These are just jokes about my uncle.
In fact, I have the best uncle
in the world, pants down,
hands down pants…
hands down.

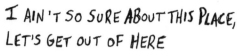

RON HAS A NERVOUS TICK

Today, a man told me that he's the
world's fastest quick-change artist.
    I said, 'Is that true?'
        She said, 'Yes.'
    I said, 'In the entire world?'
        He said, 'Yes.'
    I said, 'Really?'
        She said, 'Yes, now piss off.'

Today, I looked up the word
'digress' in the dictionary.
A dictionary that I bought in Paris.
Paris is such a beautiful city.
Especially in the springtime.
That's my favourite time of the year.
Although, I do like the Autumn.
In Canada, we call it 'the fall'.
It's a crazy world, isn't it?

• • • • • • • • • • • • • • •

Today, a man told me that
he walked here all the
way from Damascus.
  I said, 'Are you Syrian?'
    She said, 'Yes.'
  I said, 'I think you're in
  the wrong joke.'
    He got dressed and left.

There's a slim chance
my sister's anorexic.

• • • • • • • • 𝐏𝐃 • • • • • • •

I'm a very fortunate man.
I've got a wonderful career
and an amazing wife, who has
given me three incredible…
blowjobs.

Some women just don't
like giving blowjobs,
no matter how much
you sugar-coat it.

My girlfriend, who thinks
that I'm repulsed by her
vagina, has dumped me.
I won't go into it.

JACK ISN'T OUT OF THE WOODS' YET

• • • • • • • • • • • • • • • •

Today, I spent an hour scraping
dog shit off my shoe.
    No, I watched *Loose Women*.
        Same thing.

I like my women the way
I like my skis: rented…
with a little wax on their bottom.

In bed, I like to spoon.
        Anyone else do heroin?

• • • • • • • PD • • • • • • •

. . . .

Lazy? Don't get me started.

I am lazy.
      Instead of a threesome,
            I sleep with a schizophrenic.

My sister thinks
she's schizophrenic,
            and she's not alone.

      When it comes to schizophrenia,
            I for one… and one for I.

. . . . PD . . . .

· · · · · · · · · · · · · · · · ·

Sadly, because I travel so
much, I have not been present
for any of my children's...
                    conceptions.

        Fortunately, I've been
        there for all of their births,
        which is fantastic,
        because I love black babies.

Hey, wait a minute.
    I didn't finish my digress joke.

· · · · · · · PD · · · · · · ·

**DOUG'S FIRST ENCOUNTER
WITH LAWN ORNAMENTS**

• • • • • • • • • • • • • • • • •

The more I travel, the more I learn about different cultures. I was recently in Bangkok. Did you know that in Bangkok it's considered rude to display the bottom of your feet towards someone?

> Yet shoving a Coke bottle up my ass was okay with them.

Every time I eat Egyptian food, afterwards I always falafel.

Why do I do puns about Egyptian food? Just be-couscous.

> Come on, where's your sense of hummus?

• • • • • •  • • • • • •

· · · · · · · · · · · · · · · · ·

I recently flew to Belfast.
During the flight, I played
keepy-uppy with a football for
about five minutes, then
I couldn't do it anymore so I got
drunk and punched a woman.
    I received a hero's welcome
at George Best airport.

Did you know that in Turkey it's
considered rude to blow your nose
into a tissue in public?
    Yet shoving a Coke bottle up
my ass was okay with them.

· · · · · · · · PD · · · · · · · ·

SOME PREPARATION IS REQUIRED
BEFORE ART IMITATES LIFE

Know who really gives
kids a bad name?
Posh and Becks.

Posh and Becks.
Or as I like to call them:
Thick and Thin.

In an effort to improve his
looks, Wayne Rooney had a
hair transplant. It's official,
you CAN polish a turd.

I don't do a 15 minute impression of a urologist walking away from a patient any more, because it was taking the piss.

My impression of a haemophiliac shopping:
'Can I help you sir?'
'No, I'm just bruising.'

My impression of a Saudi Arabian bicycle thief:
'Look everyone, no hands.'

. . . .

There are too many bad parents
in the world. That's why I'm
seriously considering adoption.
People will say to me 'But Stewart,
you're too old to be adopted.'

I have a dog named Smooth Link.
Speaking of dogs...

...Parents have differing
views when it comes to dogs.
  When I was a little boy, my mom
  and dad said that we could get
  a puppy and, if we hated it, we
  could just abandon it.
    My foster parents however...

. . . . PD . . . .

I'm going to talk about
my childhood, so get out
your tissues, because
you're probably going to...
masturbate.

I stopped breast feeding at five.
How was your day?

After hearing that my real
parents were budgies, I couldn't
look at myself in the mirror.

THE WORLD'S FIRST 3D JOKE

I'm very tired today.
It's my own fault, last night
I got into a staring match with
a guy with two glass eyes.

I'd like to talk about something
that's close to my heart.
My pancreas.

It's my father who taught me
the importance of recycling.
I remember the first time he
took me to a recycling plant.
I remember swimming back
to shore thinking...

My oldest brother is an
expert on eclipses.
    I hated growing up in his shadow.

    My other brother, who is an
    expert on erectile dysfunction,
            is now semi-retired.

I suffer from premature ejaculation.
Hell, I get off quicker than an Italian
    captain on a sinking ship.

Today, while trying to remove
some creases from my trousers
I accidently flattened my scrotum.
            Ah, the ironing.

The first time I ever heard the
term wishful thinking used,
was by the late Peter Andre.

One of the 329 things that I hate
about Peter Andre is the fact that
he's not even British. We don't need
any foreign entertainers here in
Britain, thank you very much.

Some of you might have picked
up on the irony in that joke.
Peter Andre was actually born
in Britain, like the rest of us.

I am Canadian, although I truly do feel British because both of my parents are... alcoholics.

As everyone knows, having read my autobiography, I hate presumptuous people.

Ever take a shit so big, you needed a midwife?

When something goes wrong,
I hate the fact that my kids will
always blame someone else.
　　　They get that from their mom.

I get my tendency to
gouge from my mother.
I've got my father's eyes.

After my father passed away,
my uncle took me under his wing.
He never explained why he wore
that costume. Said he could
always get a seat on the bus.
His feathers used to tickle my nuts.

SERGEANT, I ARRESTED THIS MAN FOR IMPERSONATING A POLICE OFFICER

I respectfully admit that
my wife wears the trousers.
Mostly because of her cankles.

I call my wife doll face
because she's so pretty.
And, she's missing an eye.

I think we were both on
bumper cars, when I first
caught my wife's eye.

My wife and I met in a sushi
restaurant and last week we
went back for old time's sake.

I know people call me
egotistical behind my back,
    I can see them in the mirror.

My wife said to me
'If you looked up the word
vain in the dictionary,
you'd see your picture.'
    No I didn't.
        What the hell am I
        going to do with 48
        dictionaries?

I still can't believe I was named
sadomasochist of the year.
                    Somebody pinch me.

I was also named asthmatic
of the year although I don't
like to blow my own trumpet.

        Helping my daughter find her lost
            gerbil was a pain in the ass.

There's an old saying:
'You don't know what you've
got until it's gone' and I've never
realised that more than this
very moment because this
joke used to have a punchline.

My grade three maths teacher
used to always laugh at me and
call me stupid and say that I
would never amount to anything.
And for that grade three maths
teacher I have but two words:
'Who's laughing now?'

I'm getting old and my
body is starting to fail me.
The other night I was in a
restaurant and I couldn't
read the menu.
                    Oh, and I shit myself.

Even though I'm getting old,
I still want to challenge myself.
I want to do things that not
many people have done.
I want to swim with wild dolphins,
          I want to sky dive,
                    I want to laugh at a
                    Lenny Henry joke.

133

I used to be a motorcycle courier.
Those things are heavy.

I used to be a pantomime horse.
I quit while I was a head.

I used to sell loose onions,
til I got the sack.

I used to be a sarcastic high
jump coach: 'Get over it.'

I used to be a plastic surgeon,
which raised a few eyebrows.
Then it went tits up.

I started a VD clinic
from scratch.

I used to work in produce,
which wasn't exactly rocket salad.

How many years did I
work in a haunted house?
              You'll be surprised.

I used to work in China
repairing typewriters.
          I didn't like the job,
          but I met lots of characters.

Tired of my ridiculous puns,
my wife left me for a fisherman.
                    I was gutted.

I'm still reeling.
          She was quite the catch.
                    I miss Annette.

No, she left me for a Star Wars
enthusiast. I felt Solo.

          No, she left me for a classical
          musician. I can't Handel it.

No, she left me for a Holocaust
denier. I still can't believe it.

No, she left me for a depressed
martial artist. I still kick myself.

No, she left me for
a dyslexic astrologer.
I went to pieces.

No, she left me for a weatherman.
She'll be mist.

No, she left me for a bungee
salesman. She'll be back.

No, she left me for
an electrician.
Bitch.

138

• • • • • • • • • • • • • • • • •

Did you know that most
Americans pray before they eat?
          Can you imagine praying
          eighteen times a day?

I did that joke in America,
and they found it offensive.
     Yet, shoving a Coke bottle up
     my ass was okay with them.

          My dad's a pessimistic alcoholic.
               To him the glass is empty.

Is pessimism hereditary?
               Probably.

• • • • • • • 🅿️ • • • • • • •

My wife and I always
argue over money.
I prefer the peso.

I drove with my wife and kids
from John o'Groats all the way
to Land's End.
I wouldn't recommend it,
they're horrible people.

If dermatologists went on strike
would they be replaced by scabs?

ONCE THEY FIGURED OUT HOW TO
USE SCISSORS, THE REST WAS EASY
FOR RUSTY AND MR SNOWBALL

I'm a member of an organization
called Chronic Masturbators.
Now, if you'll excuse me.

My mother won a nasty
custody battle, which is why
I was raised by my father.

The good news is, I received
an unexpected discount on
a tattoo I had done.
The bad news is, tattooed
on my left buttock are the
words 'I Worship Satin'.

Why did I never become
a proctologist? I could
never put my finger on it.

I went for aromatherapy today,
the aromatherapist walked
into the room, farted, and said,
'That'll be fifty pounds'.
                    Aromatherapy stinks.

Most women giggle whenever
they see me naked and I'd sell
my fifth testicle to find out why.

**ART CLASS AT THE SCHOOL
FOR THE HARD OF HEARING**

My manic depressive
buddy was attacked by
a bi-polar bear today.

All seventeen of my doctors say
I have an addictive personality.

It's three beavers past a moose eh?
  Sorry, I'm still on Canadian time.

I believe in subliminal suggestion.
How about you cocksuckers?

I still go to the Orient for
my gunpowder and spices.
Call me old fashioned.

I think opposites attract.
My wife agrees.

Women are attracted to
foreign men. I've heard that
at least *uno*, *dos*, *tres* times.

I hate gossip, ask anyone.

I'm somewhat ashamed to
mention the fact that I'm
wearing a colostomy bag.
Oh, it's not mine.
I'm not a weirdo, I just find
the warmth comforting.

I've never been susceptible
to peer pressure.
      If that's okay with you?

I had a penis reduction, again.
         Third time lucky.

When my twin brother
nearly asked me to be his best man,
I was beside myself.

I caught my wife sleeping
    with the invisible man.
    Couldn't see it coming.

Incest is relatively frowned upon.

Someone broke into my flat
and stole my thesaurus.
Anyone that would steal
another's thesaurus is a real...
um...ah...

They also stole my calculator,
which doesn't add up.

FILM CRICKETS

150

Not having fog lights is
a mist opportunity.

I used to sell dining room
chairs… under the table.

I heard that my sister's
into bestiality.
Well I'll be a
monkey's uncle.

'Gimme Shelter' was an
anti-war song written
by the Rolling Stones,
who opposed the Battle of Hastings.

I was accused of stealing
hundreds of letters.
My sentence is tomorrow.

I would kill to win
the Nobel Peace Prize.

I've had twenty-seven
fiancées, which some people
find engaging.

Does anyone else like
the taste of squirrel?
    I knew I was going out on a limb.

Just because my wife made me
give up cock fighting doesn't
mean that I'm hen pecked.

People who never thought I
wanted children need only see
me playing with Drib and Drab.

My grandpa wrote that
I was a sexual deviant
in a letter I came across.

A defence lawyer's
final statement should
never include the words
'blah, blah, blah.'

My wife hates it when people
speak on her behalf.

Italians communicate
with the spirit world by
way of the Luigi board.

My brother is a therapist
and a driving instructor.
His speciality is reverse psychology.

I used to undress my
wife with my eyes.
Until I scratched my retina
on her bra strap.

My wife has narcolepsy.
She falls asleep whenever
she sees an undercover cop.

I found an old pack of Polos,
            still in mint condition.

367

I was late arriving home for dinner the other night and my wife was furious. She called me a selfish, egotistical, narcissistic jerk. I asked her what that last one meant and she said 'In Greek mythology, Narcissus was a man who saw his reflection in water, fell in love with it and stared at it for so long that he starved to death.' She asked me where I had been for so long. I told her that I was at the pond and that I was famished.

The group most downloaded
by dyslexics is ABBA.

I used to drive fifty miles
a day to plant trees.
Each day, I'd take
a different route.

I come from a long line
of tree planters.

I recently overcame my
fear of escalators.
It was a twelve-step program.

Four out of ten people
are used in surveys.
        Six are not.

Recently separated conjoined
twins are my cousins.
                Once removed.

My uncle just bought a prosthetic.
                Second hand.

    I wanted to join a self-help group
        but no one would drive me.

Crime in lifts is on the rise.

~~(SV)~~ IS Pillow theft ~~is~~ down?

People accuse me of
being too organised,
which I categorically deny.

My parents taught me everything
except good manners.
I don't know how to thank them.

Shots were fired at an art studio.
                    Details are sketchy.

I think some customs officers
are borderline rude.

            Everyone in the world thinks
            I exaggerate too much.

I've started to eat more sensibly.
            For years I've been using
            a spatula and whisk.

I'm constantly delayed
at airport security.
            Damn these buns of steel.

            Two words on how the Amish
      bank robbers were tracked down:
                        horse droppings.

I went to a silent auction.
                  Bought a mime.

My psychic won ten grand
in the lottery. Happy medium.

PETTY CRIMINAL WAYNE
OF NO FIXED ADDRESS

I still haven't quite made it to my
depth perception therapy class.

Asked when could I start
my job as an estimator I said,
'Um, tomorrow?... June?'

I've written over
five thousand books on
how to start a library.

Woke up with a stiff neck.
My wife says she hopes it spreads.

The number of twins being born has doubled.

My wife's neighbour's sister's boyfriend's hairdresser's cousin thinks I'm too complex.

I get my repetitiveness from my great great great great great grandfather.

I'LL TELL YOU WHY I THINK YOU'RE BORED WITH ME. THERE'S A THOUGHT BUBBLE WITH BIKINI CLAD GIRLS ABOVE YOUR HEAD

Women always have heavy luggage.
I rest my case.

I love blind dates, 'cause you can stare at their tits.

I have an aunt and uncle who met on a blind date 51 years ago and just recently celebrated their 50th wedding anniversary. On their way home from their anniversary party, a drunk driver crossed over into their lane, smashing into their car and killing them instantly.
Let that be a lesson to all of you.
Blind dates don't always work out.

With all the ointments on the market today, it's easy to make a rash decision.

My wife is a striking beauty.
She works for London Underground.

I was just telling my shoelace washer that I'll never let success change me.

I'll always be a socialist, or my name's not Stewart Francis™.

The best form of advertising
is 'word of mouth'. Pass it on.

Are vegetarians opposed
to track meets?

Experts say illiteracy is hereditary,
but will they put it in writing?

Have you ever had a pimple
in a disgusting place,
like Barnstable?

I want conjoined twins to be
separated as much as the next guy.

When my parents divorced,
my father fought for joint custody.
                        He got my elbows.

Violence is not the answer.
            My father sure beat
            that into my head.

I was accused of watching too
many reality shows by my ✖ wife.

CUSTER'S LAST TAN

I have never been in a failed relationship. I currently have 15 girlfriends, 3 wives and a Swedish boyfriend named Lars.

Everyone in Hollywood is vain. Even hunchbacks have implants.

If I could change just one thing about myself, it would be for me to be less self-centred. How about you, what would you change about me?

My uncle, who invented
disappearing ink, died recently.
I was in his will... briefly.

A proctologist recognised me
after TWENTY-FIVE YEARS.
Talk about anally retentive.

Philosophers say the worst
place to live is the past.
Then Barnstable.

Clichés are a dime a dozen.

You can take the boy out of
the country, but, you should
ask his folks first.

What do deaf people play it by?

I used to have a permanent limp.

Mother would make me eat a
salad then go to bed at 5pm.
She was a strict vegetarian.

**HAVING A LAZY EYE WAS A BLESSING
TO SECURITY GUARD BILL**

I'm the King of underachievers. Actually, I'm the Earl of underachievers.

I'm an underachiever 24-6.

Next time someone who always brags about how smart their pets are visits, put a knife and fork beside your pet's bowl.

Degenerative hips are on my father's side.

Blind women love sleeping with
Leonardo DiCaprio, or is it just me?

A JELLY-LIKE FLUID.
There, I'm not afraid to say
what's on my mind.

While on my way to my
Alzheimer's support group,
I saw something that
I'll never remember.

I don't like being in a confined
space with Germans.
I'm Klaustrophobic.

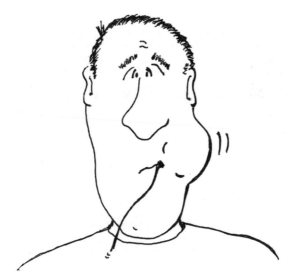

**RETIRED GOALKEEPER JIM STILL
HAS CAT-LIKE REFLEXES**

The French are very chauvinistic. Here's my impression of a French boy lost in a cave.

'PAPA (papa, papa, papa)...
MAMA (papa, papa, papa).'

When my school orientation meeting was cancelled I didn't know which way to turn.

One word can change a horrible news story into a happy news story. See if you can spot the word here:

'Shortly after the boat sank, the bodies of fifty-four paedophiles washed up on shore.'

Here are some
photos of my
beautiful wife,
Paige Turner

Paige Turner

Paige Turner

183

Paige Turner

Paige Turner

185

I once did a show for a group
of squirrel enthusiasts.
   I had them eating out of my hand.

I once did a show in a haystack.
      You could hear a pin drop.

            My ventriloquist skills
            speak for themselves.

Every time I visit my family plot
at the cemetery I realise that I
come from a long line of smokers.

Most gravediggers
are deep thinkers.

My vagueness is like
a cucumber.

I used to talk in the past tense.
Thankfully, those days are over.

Why do my family
always dress so casually?
It's in our genes.

• • • • • • • • • • • • • • • • •

I did something nice today, I held
the elevator door open for a spastic.
Sorry, that's an inappropriate word…
in Britain you say 'lift'.

There's an anti-conformist
convention. Been there,
didn't buy the t-shirt.

Fans of oral sex
look up to me.

To save our marriage, my wife and
I have taken up square dancing.
I think we've turned a corner.

• • • • • • •  • • • • • •

I used to recycle calendars.
Those were the days.

Today, a horse said to me, 'Hey
buddy, why the long… penis?'

Doctors are trying to find
a cure for pessimism.
I don't like their chances.

I've learned two things in life.
The second, is to never cut corners.

Today, a midget told me
that my wife wants me out
of the house immediately.
                 That's short notice.

Once when I was a lawyer
a judge called me unprofessional,
so I threw my slippers at her.

When I was a taxi driver, I'd regret
the fact that I could never identify
fare jumpers. Still, I can't look back.

LLOYD, THE HARD OF HEARING WIZARD

Every four seconds,
someone in the world is the
victim of fear mongering…
you could be next.

Don't tell the man who invented
Viagra that you think he's amazing.
It'll just go to his head.

Did you know that that
ball launcher gadget was
invented by a dog?
I know, it sounds far-fetched.

I hate Scrabble so much,
        I can't put it into words.

I've been making puns about
        Motown music ever since
        I was three... four tops.

I will never do a pun
about crack cocaine.
 Put that in your pipe and smoke it.

Concerned about my eyesight,
        I saw a doctor today,
        which was a relief.

I don't believe in astrology,
which is typical for a Capricorn.

Insecure people need
constant reassuring.
Am I right?

Working in a dark warehouse
full of dildos gave me the willies.

I've had a good
experience with
proctologists,
on the whole.

Do people think I'm too queasy?
I haven't the faintest idea.

Is my French wife
into golden showers?
Oui.

Once, when I was a
security guard, a man asked
if he could pee on my wrist.
I said, 'Not on my watch.'

196

I do puns about Canadian wildlife.
Bear with me.

I'm Canadian, but if people
think I'm Russian... Soviet.

My impotent brother
is a graffiti artist.
Blanksy.

The instant my wife and I put
our mats down we start to argue.
Bickering Yoga.

I'll never do puns about arthritis.
Fingers crossed.

'Any man who lives his life in
accordance to a book is a fool.'
Luke 317.

I can say 'No one likes
a show off' in forty-three
languages.

Last night I went to a karaoke bar
that didn't play any '70s music...
at first I was afraid.

The grass is greener on
the other side of the fence,
explained my neighbour as
he returned my sprinkler.

Why was I fired from the AA?
            Don't get me started.

Of the twenty-seven
students in my maths class,
I was the only one who failed.
            What are the odds of that,
                    one in a million?

WITH HER NEIGHBOUR BEING SO QUIET
AND FRIENDLY, HELEN DECIDES TO CALL
THE POLICE BEFORE HE GOES BERSERK
AND KILLS SOMEONE

So what if I can't spell Armugeddon,
it's not the end of the world.

What's the deal with trainspotters?
I counted **27** of the losers today.
My record's **41**.

My hobbies include
re-wiring microwave ovens
and meeting firemen.

My dad has a weird hobby,
he collects empty bottles,
which sounds so much
better than alcoholic.

I was fired as a Boy Scout leader.
I wasn't prepared for that.

I made a career out of
stealing the aerodynamic
devices off cars.
Spoiler alert.

My wife's been putting in too
many hours at the fracture clinic.
She needs a break.

I had a fantastic career
making bouquets,
but I threw it away.

CHANTING AT STALE MILK FOR TWENTY
MINUTES MADE NANCY REALISE THAT SHE WAS
PROBABLY GOING TO TOO MANY HEN PARTIES

At first, I didn't believe
my father stole from his
job as a lollipop man,
          but all the signs were there.

People can be so judgmental.
Yes, my father went bankrupt,
selling polo hammers
that are too short.
          I just wish some people would
          get off their high horses.

Through no fault of
his own, my uncle crashed
his car into a lemon tree.
He's still bitter and twisted.
His head's the shape of Florida.
          Terrible state.

I've met some cynical people
in my twenty-eight years.

Did I already do my déjà vu joke?

Where I was once opposed,
I'm now in favour of fat people
being buried together...
the plot thickens.

Two of my best friends
are named William Hill...
What are the odds?

I was standing in the park
today wondering, 'Why do
Frisbees appear larger the
closer they get?'
And then it hit me.

Always leave an
audience wanting...

FOOTNOTES

Toronto, Canada

Caithness, Scotland

Ho Chi Minh City, Vietnam

Hong Kong, PRC

Sydney, Australia

Koh Booboo, Thailand

Ibiza, Spain

Algonquin Park, Canada

INDEX

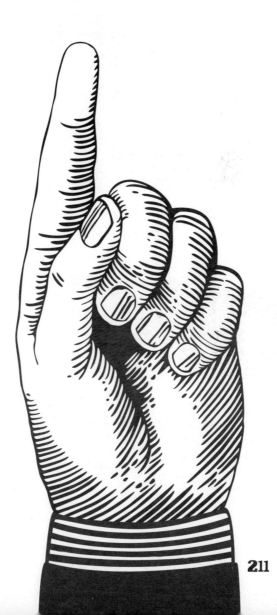

APPENDIX

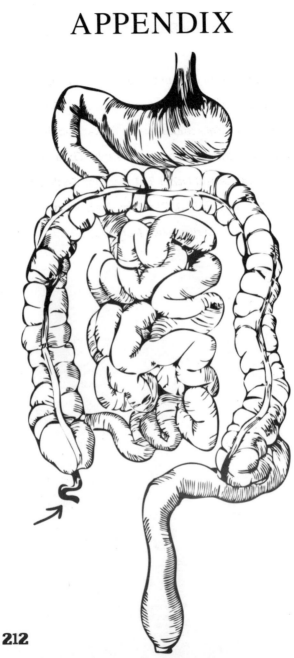

Also by Stewart Francis

The History of Quiet Stereos: Volume One

Nightmares: The Study of Nocturnal Horses

The Complete Idiots' Guide to Name-calling

Funeral Etiquette: When's the Right Time to Fart?

Sex Addicts and Other Things That Don't Exist

War Criminal: The Tony Blair Story

Living With Narcolep

ABOOT THE AUTHOR

Stewart is a friendly Canadian
who hates stereotypes…

and seal pups.